For my parents, with love and thanks for a beautiful garden of childhood memories... C.R.

For Caroline, Mike, Amanda and everyone at Templar. With special thanks to my parents for their tremendous help and encouragement...I.A.

A TEMPLAR BOOK

First published in the UK in 1997 by Templar Publishing

Distributed in the UK by Ragged Bears Ltd.,
Ragged Appleshaw, Andover, Hampshire SP11 9HX.

Devised and produced by The Templar Company plc
Pippbrook Mill, London Road, Dorking, Surrey RH4 IJE.

Illustrations copyright © 1997 by Ian Andrew
This edition copyright © 1997 by The Templar Company plc

Designed by Mike Jolley

ISBN 1-898784-09-4

Printed in Italy

TEMPLAR
PUBLISHING

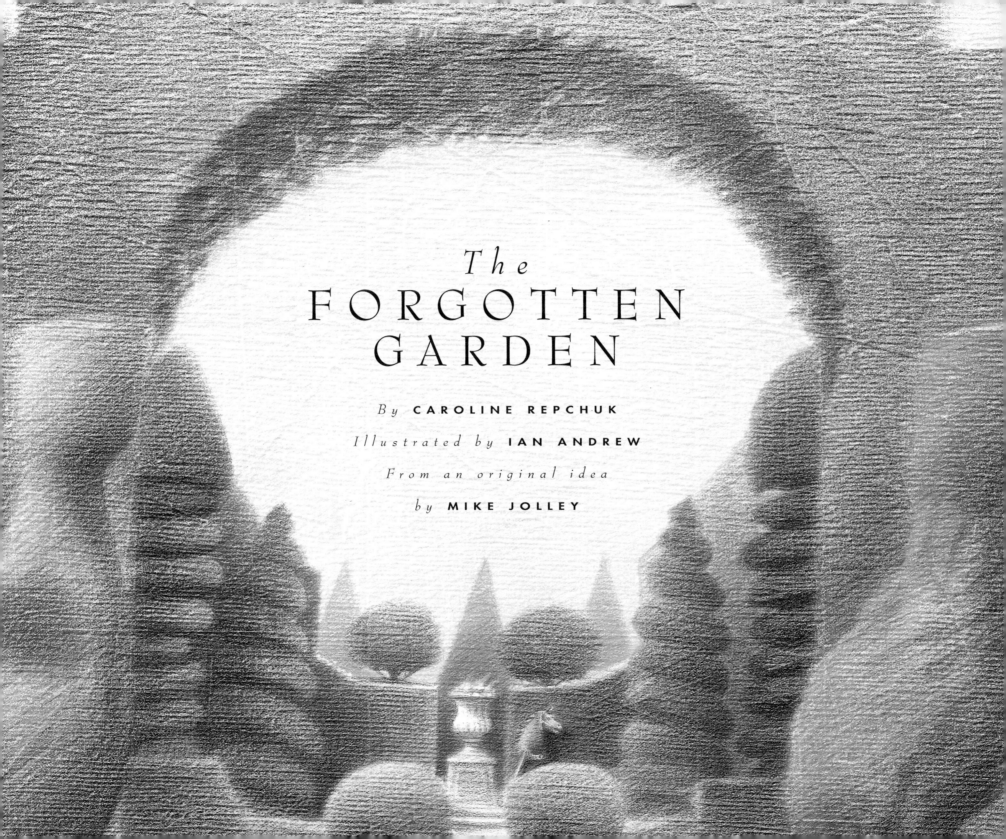

The
FORGOTTEN
GARDEN

By **CAROLINE REPCHUK**

Illustrated by **IAN ANDREW**

From an original idea

by **MIKE JOLLEY**

The old man stood before the rusted gates
and memories danced around him
like the leaves at his feet.

He stood, frozen in time, and recalled a garden so beautiful
it had charmed the birds from the skies and
the beasts from the fields beyond.

Now beauty stood strangled by neglect.
Gone were the rustlings of life,
the blaze of colour and the birdsong.

ADAM GREEN
GARDENER

In a far corner of the garden he stepped inside
the crumbling, colourless greenhouse.

The dust unsettled
    as he passed his fingers over familiar surfaces.

The man took up the timeworn shears,
  and a shaft of sunlight fell across his back.

A shape beckoned to him from deep within the sprawling hedge.

Snip, snip, snip.

    The new-oiled shears snapped to attention.

And as he clipped...

... the sleeping garden stirred and blinked, it yawned and stretched, and began to come alive once more.

Whisperings
came from every corner.

Mysterious forms enticed him
        from far inside the tangled bushes.

The creaking shears flashed
as he fashioned a fox from a fir tree...

They sparked as he spurred
a stallion from a spruce…

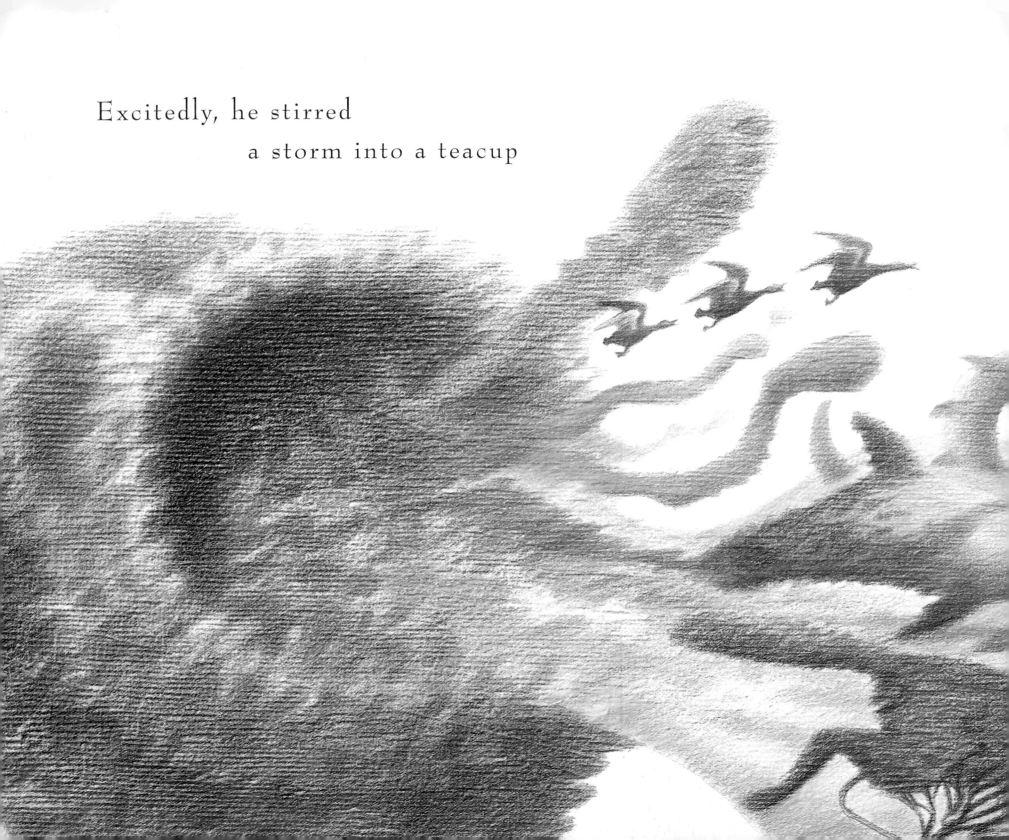

Excitedly, he stirred

a storm into a teacup

and snipped a ship
into shape...

Lovingly he cleared

the mouth of a fountain,

and water poured forth
to quench the thirst of a time-parched pool.

He swept away a lifetime of leaves,
        rolling the years back as he did so...

IN LOVING MEMORY OF
ADAM GREEN
1879 - 1918
AND
FLORA GREEN
1883 - 1928
BELOVED PARENTS
OF BEN GREEN

High above him the mighty bird circled,
before swooping low and alighting
in the garden once more.

Behind him followed a whole
host of songbirds, who
filled the air with a
symphony of sound.

For a moment he paused,
and looked around him.

Flowers now sprang
to adorn every corner
and gleaming berries
bejewelled the trees.

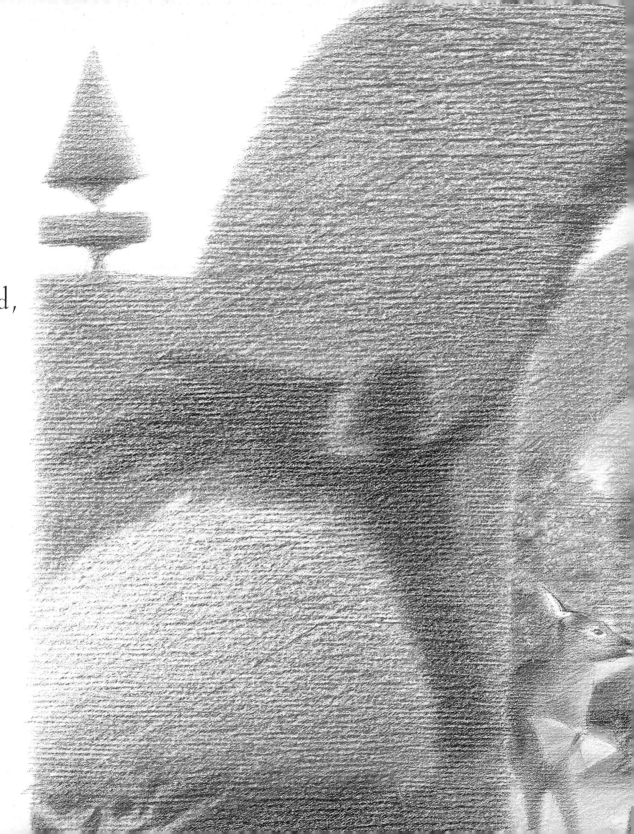

They shimmered in the
sunlight as the circle
of life revolved.

He stood once more
in a garden so beautiful
that it had charmed
the birds from the skies
and the beasts from
the fields beyond…

And he was
no longer alone…